FERGUS

THE FARMYARD DOG

To Natalie, Zara, Chloe, Holly and Jamie

Phototypeset by Spooner Graphics, NW5
for the publishers, Piccadilly Press Ltd.,
5 Castle Road, London NW1 8PR

A catalogue record for this book is available from the British Library

Tony Maddox is British and lives in Worcestershire with his wife. He illustrates greetings cards as well as books. Piccadilly Press published his first picture book, SPIKE THE SPARROW WHO COULDN'T SING!

FERGUS THE FARMYARD DOG

Tony Maddox

Piccadilly Press, London

Fergus the farmyard dog lay in the warm sunshine and tried to sleep. But all he could hear was the *Cluck, Cluck, Cluck* of the hens in the yard.

And the *Quack, Quack, Quack* of the ducks by the pond.

FEED

Then he heard the *Squeak* . . . *Squeak*
. . . *Squeak* of . . .
Fergus looked around.
What was making that noise?

The sheep in the meadow were going
Baa, Baa, Baa.

The pigs in their pen were going
Oink, Oink, Oink.
Squeak . . . Squeak . . . Squeak . . .
What could it be?

He ran to the cowshed.
The cows went
Moo, Moo, Moo.
Squeak . . . Squeak . . .
Squeak . . .

What's that noise?

He ran to the paddock. The donkey went *Hee Haw, Hee Haw*!

Fergus sat down, raised both ears and listened as hard as he could.

Cluck, Cluck, Quack, Quack,
Squeak . . .
There it was!
Baa, Baa, Oink, Oink, Squeak . . .
There it was again!
Moo, Moo, Hee Haw, Squeak!

It seemed to be coming from the
garden behind the farmhouse.
Squeak . . . Squeak . . . Squeak . . .
Fergus crept up and peeped through
the open gateway to see . . .

. . . . Farmer Bob asleep in
the old garden seat
which hung from
the apple tree.

As it swung slowly to and fro it went . . .
Squeak . . . Squeak . . . Squeak!

'Woof, Woof!' went Fergus.
Farmer Bob woke up with a start.
'What's wrong, Fergus?' he said.
'Woof, Woof, Woof!' went Fergus again.

Then Farmer Bob noticed the squeak. 'Is that what's wrong?' he said. 'Soon fix that! A spot of oil should do the trick.'

When the squeaky parts had been oiled, Farmer Bob sat back on the seat and Fergus jumped up beside him.

In no time at all the two of them were asleep.

Brrrrrrrrrrrrrr. Brrrrrrrrrrrrrr!

What's THAT noise?

PRINTED IN BELGIUM BY
proost
INTERNATIONAL BOOK PRODUCTION